Quincy, The Cat of La Mancha

By
Dominic R. Villari

Quincy was a brave cat who lived in a town called La Mancha. He liked to wear a purple blanket knitted by his owner Nia.

Quincy was very loyal to Nia. He protected her yard from pests.

Quincy scared away the birds that pecked at the windows.

Quincy caught the mice that dug holes in the yard.

One day Quincy could not find Nia.

Quincy decided he would go on a quest to find Nia and rescue her.

He saw his friend Sancho the squirrel in the yard. "Sancho," called out Quincy. "We are going on a quest."

"A quest?" asked Sancho. "I was just about to take a nap."

"There will be time for sleeping later," said Quincy. "Nia is missing and we must find her."

Sancho sighed. "I will go with you, Quincy. There are many bees in the yard today. The buzzing is keeping me awake anyway."

"Fetch me my armor, Sancho," said Quincy.

"Where is your armor?" asked Sancho.

"My armor is right there," answered Quincy. He pointed to a pile of objects.

"Hand me my chest plate, said Quincy."

"But this is a pie pan," said Sancho.

"No, that is my chest plate," said Quincy.

He tied the pie pan around his chest. "Now hand me my helmet."

"This is a pasta bowl," said Sancho.

"No, that is my helmet," said Quincy. He put the bowl on his head.

The bowl had two holes in it just big enough to fit Quincy's ears. "Now hand me my lance."

"This is a fishing pole," said Sancho.

"No, that is my lance," said Quincy. He took the fishing pole from Sancho and waved it around.

"Now we are ready for our quest."

"Maybe you could chase away some of these bees," said Sancho. "Then I could take my nap."

"I have greater concerns than bees Sancho," said Quincy. "Let us begin our journey."

Quincy walked to the front yard of the house. Sancho followed close behind.

"Halt, Sancho," said Quincy. "A giant stands before us."

"That's not a giant," said Sancho. "That's the plastic windmill in the front garden."

"It is a giant," said Quincy. "Stand back, Sancho." Quincy stepped forward. He whacked the giant over the head with his lance.

"I don't think that will work," said Sancho. Just then the giant fell over with a thud.

Quincy waved his lance in the air. "I have defeated the giant. It is safe for us to continue."

"I'm tired," said Sancho. "Let's go back to the house. I'll get us some seed from the bird feeder."

"Our quest has just begun," said Quincy. "I believe we should recite the knight's code. That will lift your spirits, Sancho.

"A knight is always honorable," said Quincy. "A knight is always honorable," repeated Sancho.

"A knight is always loyal," said Quincy. "A knight is always loyal," said Sancho.

"A knight is always brave," said Quincy. "A knight is always brave," said Sancho.

"Are you ready to continue now?" asked Quincy.

"Yes," replied Sancho.

After traveling a short time they found a piece of metal on a chain. It had words and a pair of wings on it.

Quincy picked it up.

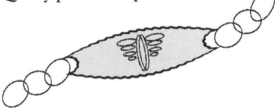

"Look Sancho," said Quincy. "A gift for Nia."

Suddenly a crow flew at Quincy's head, squawking loudly. "Give me that shiny thing," said the crow.

He picked up a stick in his beak and waved it at Quincy.

"I cannot," replied Quincy. "It is a gift for my lady, Nia ." Quincy raised his lance and waved it at the crow.

"But I plan to give it to a lady crow," said the crow, swinging the stick at Quincy. "I need it to win her love."

Quincy swung his lance against the crow's stick. "You are a very good swordsman," said Quincy. "

"But that bit of metal is no way to win your lady's heart."

"Then it is no way to win your lady's heart either," said the crow.

"I have already won my lady Nia's heart," replied Quincy. "The gift is to welcome her home. She is missing."

"I'm sorry to hear that said the crow," he stopped fighting with Quincy.

"How did you win your lady's heart then?" asked the crow.

"I earned her love with my actions," said Quincy.

"How?" asked the crow.

"A knight is always honorable," said Quincy. "A knight is always honorable," repeated Sancho.

"A knight is always loyal," said Quincy. "A knight is always loyal," said Sancho.

"A knight is always brave," said Quincy. "A knight is always brave," said Sancho.

The crow turned his head to one side and looked at Quincy.

"I need to be honorable," said the crow. "I need to be loyal. I need to be brave."

"Yes," said Quincy. "Then you will win her heart."

"I understand," said the crow. He bowed to Quincy. "Thank you," said the crow and he flew away.

"Come Sancho," said Quincy. "Let us continue our quest."

Quincy and Sancho walked for a long time. They crossed a large field. On the other side of the field they saw three cages.

There was a rabbit in the first cage. "Please sir," said the rabbit. "Let me out of this cage."

"Who has locked you in here?" asked Quincy.

"The animal catcher," said the rabbit.
"I was caught stealing from the garden."

"Stealing is not honorable," said Quincy.

"I was taking carrots to feed my family,"
said the rabbit. "Please let me out."

"Feeding your family is honorable,"
said Quincy. "But stealing is still wrong."

"You are right," said the rabbit. "I should have asked for the carrots."

"Since you have learned your lesson," said Quincy, "I will let you out."

Quincy used his lance to release the lock and set the rabbit free.

"Thank you," said the rabbit and he hopped away.

"A knight is always honorable," said Quincy.

"A knight is always honorable," said Sancho.

There was a groundhog in the second cage. "I saw you free the rabbit," said the groundhog. "Let me out too."

"Why have you been locked in this cage?" asked Quincy.

"I was digging holes through the flowers," said the groundhog. "I wanted to build my own den. I'm tired of living with my brothers and sisters."

"That was not very loyal of you," said Quincy. "Your selfishness has led you into trouble."

"You are right," said the groundhog.

"If I had stayed with my family I would not have strayed into the flower bed."

"Since you have learned your lesson," said Quincy, "I will free you from the cage." Quincy used his lance to release the lock and set the groundhog free.

"Thank you," said the groundhog and he scampered away.

"A knight is always loyal," said Quincy.

"A knight is always loyal," said Sancho.

There was a raccoon in the third cage.

"Please, oh please good knight," called the raccoon.

"I saw you free the rabbit and the groundhog. I too have learned my lesson. Set me free."

"Why are you in this cage?" asked Quincy.

"I was caught rooting through the garbage," said the raccoon. "I was looking for lost treasures."

"What lesson have you learned?" asked Quincy.

The raccoon laughed. "I have learned not to get caught next time," he said.

"Then you have learned nothing," said Quincy. " He did not free the raccoon from the cage.

The raccoon laughed again. "That is a bowl on your head," he said. "That is a fishing pole in your hand. You are wearing a pie plate on your chest. You are not a real knight"

"A knight is always brave," said Quincy.
"A knight is always brave," said Sancho.

Quincy and Sancho left the raccoon and continued their quest. They traveled until the light began to fade.

"The day is almost over," said Sancho. "And we have not completed our quest."

"You are right," said Quincy. He took off his helmet and put down his lance.

"Perhaps I am not a knight," he said.

Sancho saw that his friend looked sad.

"A knight is always honorable," said Sancho. "You always do the right thing."

He handed Quincy his helmet. Quincy put the helment back on his head.

"A knight is always loyal," said Sancho. "You have not stopped looking for Nia." Quincy picked up his lance.

"A knight is always brave," said Sancho. "You stood up to the giant, the crow and the raccoon." Quincy lifted his head.

Just as Quincy lifted his head, he saw Nia. She was on top of a table. Several men and women were standing around her. They pushed her into a large castle with glass doors.

"There is Lady Nia," he said to Sancho. "We must go before the glass doors close." They ran through the glass doors just in time.

Quincy and Sancho watched the men and women take Nia into another room. They were about to follow when a broom swept across their path.

"A giant is guarding the entrance," said Quincy.

"I think that is a janitor," said Sancho. "And he has a broom."

"His lance is no match for my own," said Quincy. He lowered his lance and charged forward.

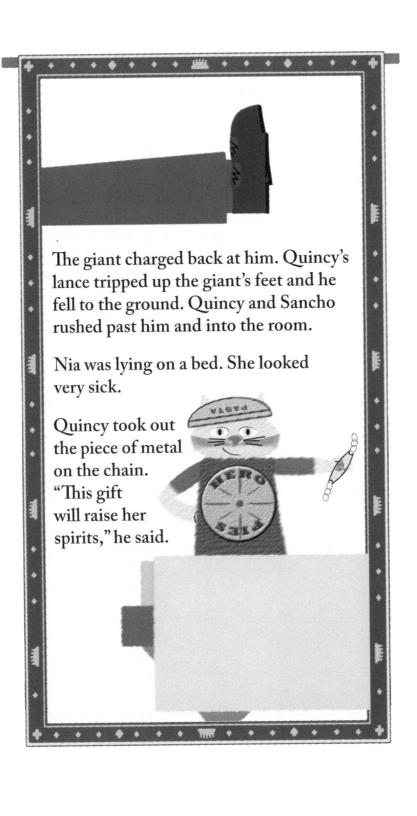

The giant charged back at him. Quincy's lance tripped up the giant's feet and he fell to the ground. Quincy and Sancho rushed past him and into the room.

Nia was lying on a bed. She looked very sick.

Quincy took out the piece of metal on the chain. "This gift will raise her spirits," he said.

Quincy jumped up onto the table. He dropped the piece of metal into Nia's hand.

One of the men picked it up.

"Look at the name on this bracelet," said the man. "It belongs to her." The man leaned over Nia and pushed a very small lance into her arm.

At first Quincy was worried but suddenly Nia woke up.

"Quincy," said Nia. "I'm so glad to see you."

"And you found my alert bracelet. That bee sting made me very sick."

"This cat is a hero," said the man.
Quincy bowed to the man and to Nia.
"But why is he wearing a pasta bowl
and a pie pan?" asked the man.

"Because Quincy is a knight," said Nia.
"He is honorable, loyal and brave."

"A knight is always honorable," said Quincy. "A knight is always honorable," repeated Sancho.

"A knight is always loyal," said Quincy. "A knight is always loyal," said Sancho.

"A knight is always brave," said Quincy. "A knight is always brave," said Sancho.

Quincy, the Cat of La Mancha